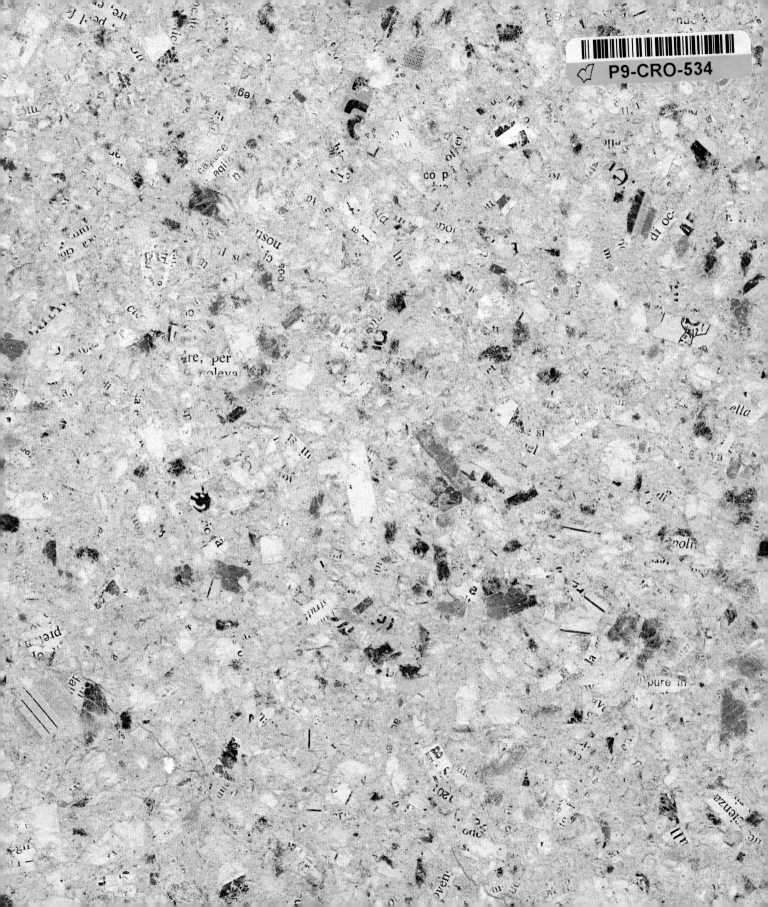

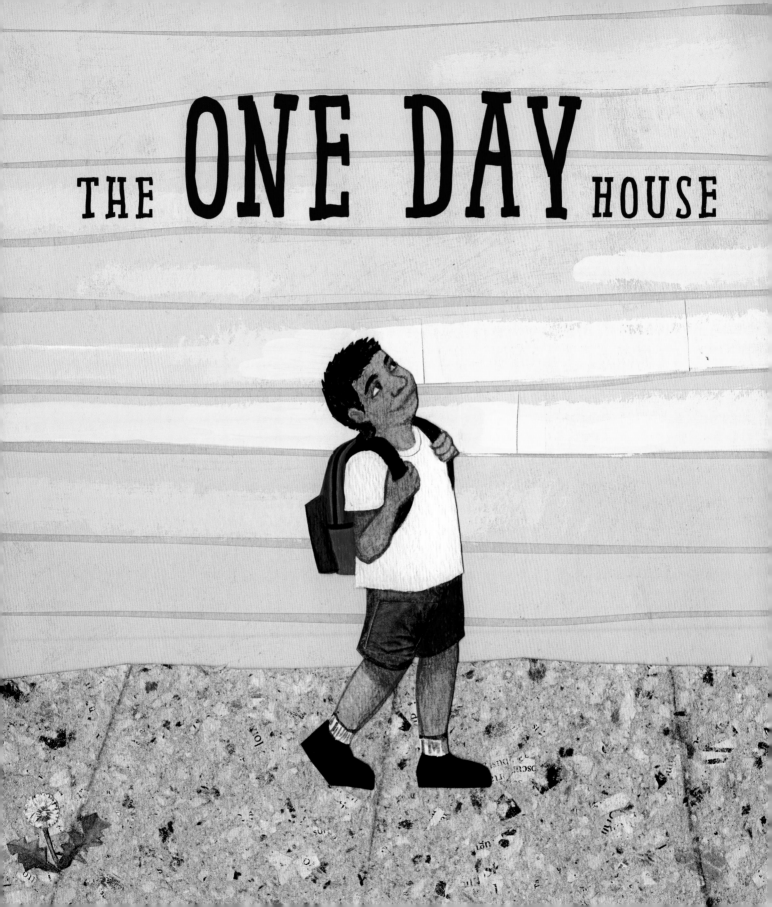

THE **ONE DAY** HOUSE

JULIA DURANGO

ILLUSTRATED BY BIANCA DIAZ

OPEN

Beauty Salon

Charlesbridge

Gigi's House →

"One day," said Wilson, "I will paint your house orange and yellow like the sun."

Gigi smiled. "I will like that. But today, you are all the sunshine I need," she said.

"One day," said Wilson, "I will fix Gigi's windows so she can open them wide and feel the breeze."

"That's a fine idea," said the ice-cream man. "Fresh air is good for the soul."

"One day," said Wilson, "I will build a fence around the yard so you can have a dog to keep you company."

"I will like that," said Gigi. "But today, I have all the company I need."

"One day," said Wilson, "I will fix the stairs so Gigi can sit on the balcony and see forever."

"That's a beautiful idea," said a passing neighbor.

"Everyone enjoys a pretty view," agreed her friend.

rope

brush

heavy ball

"One day," said Wilson, "I will fix the chimney so you can make a fire to keep you cozy."

"I will like that," said Gigi. "But today, you are all the warmth I need."

LIFE ON MARS

SNOW MAN
SUNDAE

SWIMMING POOL
LIVING ROOM

"One day," said Wilson, "I will fix the roof on Gigi's house to keep out the wind and snow."

"That's a smart idea," said the librarian. "There's nothing better than a snug house on a wintry day."

PIANO TUNING
SINGING

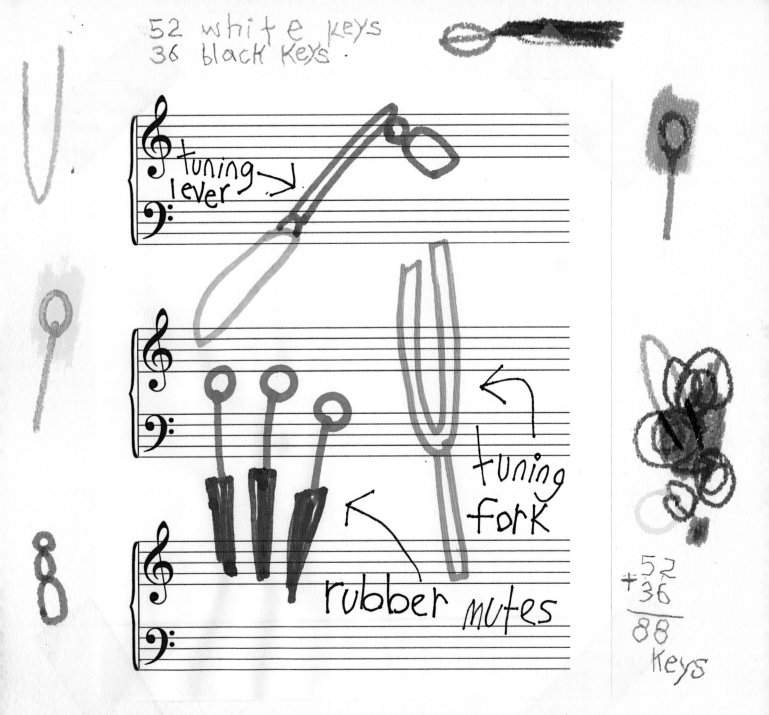

"One day," said Wilson, "I will fix your piano so you can play music again."

"I will like that," said Gigi. "But today, you are the song in my heart."

"One day," said Wilson, "I will plant a garden for Gigi so she can be surrounded by flowers."

"That's a great idea," said Wilson's teacher. "It's fun to watch things grow."

"One day," said Gigi, "is a very nice day indeed."
"One day," said Wilson, "is the best day ever."
Gigi smiled. "The very best," she agreed. "Just like you."

AUTHOR'S NOTE

The inspiration for *The One Day House* came from my local writing partner and friend, Bill Cairns. Bill, a carpenter by trade, has volunteered his time and talents for the past fifteen years to our community's annual Labor of Love event, a day each fall where hundreds of volunteers come together to help repair the homes of the elderly, disabled, and needy in eastern LaSalle County, Illinois. Roofs are patched, windows are replaced, boilers are fixed, trees are trimmed—whatever needs doing gets done. Local businesses donate building supplies, and church and charity groups work together to feed the volunteers throughout the day. It truly is a labor of love—an amazing display of human compassion and generosity at its best.

Our community isn't the first to do this, of course. Since the earliest days in America, people have come together to help their neighbors in need. From the barn raisings of American pioneers to the soup kitchens of the Great Depression to the vibrant, viral grassroots efforts of modern-day relief organizations, the can-do spirit and kindness of volunteers sparkle bright in our history.

If you wish to volunteer for a "labor of love" in your own community, check with local relief agencies and charities, or log on to United Way (www.unitedway.org) or Habitat for Humanity (www.habitat.org) to find out how you can help. Together, we can make "one day" start today!

For Bill Cairns, Tracie Vaughn Kleman, Linda Sue Park, and Suzanne Wilson,
who make this world a better place in words and deeds—J. D.
For my first-grade teacher, Ms. Charvat, who made me feel big.—B. D.

Text copyright © 2017 by Julia Durango
Illustrations copyright © 2017 by Bianca Diaz
All rights reserved, including the right of reproduction in whole or in part
    in any form. Charlesbridge and colophon are registered trademarks of
    Charlesbridge Publishing, Inc.
Published by Charlesbridge, 85 Main Street, Watertown, MA 02472
(617) 926-0329 · www.charlesbridge.com

Printed in China
(hc) 10 9 8 7 6 5 4 3 2 1

Illustrations were collaged using watercolor, gouache, and acrylic paints; india ink;
    colored pencils; crayons; markers; magazine cutouts; photo transfers;
    and handmade paper.
Display type set in Pinto NO_2 by FaceType
Text type set in Helenita by RodrigoTypo
Color separations by Colourscan Print Co Pte Ltd, Singapore
Printed by 1010 Printing International Limited in Huizhou,
    Guangdong, China
Production supervision by Brian G. Walker
Designed by Susan Mallory Sherman

Library of Congress Cataloging-in-Publication Data
Names: Durango, Julia, 1967– author. | Diaz, Bianca, illustrator.
Title: The one-day house/Julia Durango; illustrated by Bianca Diaz.
Description: Watertown, MA: Charlesbridge, [2016] | Summary: A little boy promises
    his beloved friend, an elderly lady, that one day he will fix up her old house—
    and his words inspire the other people in the neighborhood to pitch in and
    get it done.
Identifiers: LCCN 2015026863 |
ISBN 9781580897099 (reinforced for library use) | ISBN 9781607349235 (ebook) |
ISBN 9781607349242 (ebook pdf)
Subjects: LCSH: Dwellings—Juvenile fiction. | Neighbors—Juvenile fiction. |
    Helping behavior—Juvenile fiction. | Communities—Juvenile fiction. |
    CYAC: Dwellings—Fiction. | Neighbors—Fiction | Helpfulness—Fiction. |
    Voluntarism—Fiction. | Community life—Fiction.
Classification: LCC PZ7.D9315 On 2016 | DDC [E]—dc23 LC record available at
http://lccn.loc.gov/2015026863

31192021294580